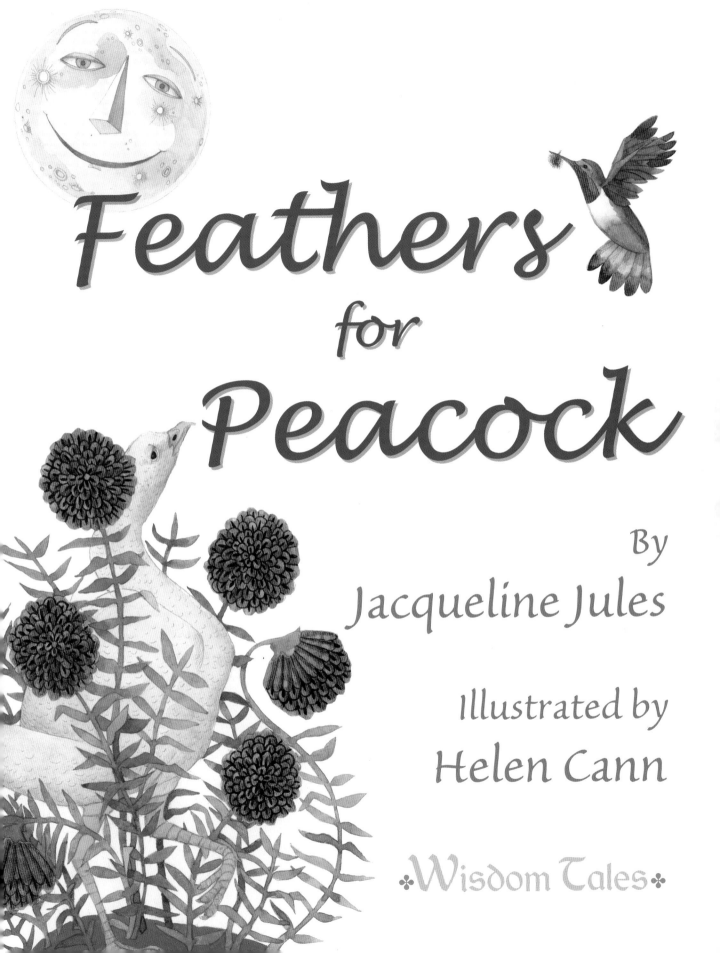

Feathers
for
Peacock

By
Jacqueline Jules

Illustrated by
Helen Cann

❖Wisdom Tales❖

L ong ago, when the world was new, Peacock did
not have the beautiful feathers he has now.
Peacock was naked. In winter, he shivered
and sniffled. He was so cold, he crawled into a cave
and hid under a pile of leaves to keep warm.

His friends went underground, too. All birds were

Fox

Snail

Turtle

Fish

Armadillo

"It's not fair," Eagle grumbled. "Foxes have fur. Turtles have shells. Birds need warm coats, too."

"This is true," Hawk agreed. "But what can we do?"

"I have heard," Eagle said, "that the full moon is very wise. Let's ask her advice."

"But we must wait till spring," Hawk said, "when the snow melts and we can go outside."

Slowly, the winter months passed. The air warmed and flowers pushed up from the earth.

Eagle and Hawk walked from one cave to another. "Come to a meeting at the full moon!" they called.

Birds with small beaks told birds with long beaks. Plump birds told skinny birds. Short birds told tall birds, until everyone knew to come.

Except Peacock. He was buried under a pile of leaves, sound asleep.

On the night of the meeting, birds of every shape and size gazed up at the sky with hopeful eyes. The moon looked down and gasped.

"Oh, dear! You're naked!"

"And cold!" they cried.

"I will help you," the moon promised. "Tomorrow at dawn, when the sun and I share the sky, rub against the plants and flowers. You will be clothed."

The birds waited, huddled together, until the first rays of light.

Parrot hopped over to a tulip. Flamingo lifted her long neck into cherry blossoms.

Duck was so excited that he rubbed his head in the grass and his body against a tree.

Instantly, the birds had new feathery coats the
same colors as the plants they had chosen.

"Let's have a party!" Owl hooted, showing off new brown feathers.

"Absolutely!" Raven flapped his shiny black wings.

The birds celebrated the whole day. They danced. They sang. They played the drums. The music echoed all the way to the cave where Peacock was still sleeping under a pile of leaves.

Hearing the music, he finally woke up and hurried to the party. There he saw his friends covered in warm colorful feathers.

Tears dripped down Peacock's face as the sun went down and the moon rose.

Turkey noticed first. "Look at Peacock. He's still naked!"

The birds stared at Peacock, trembling in the chilly spring night.

"He missed his chance," Swan sighed. "The moon told us to rub against the plants at dawn."

"He could try it anyway," Hummingbird suggested.

Peacock hugged a bush. Nothing happened. He was as naked as ever.

"We can't leave him like that," Robin said.
"No, we can't," Blue Jay agreed.
She pulled a bright blue feather from her
own body and offered it to Peacock.
Parrot followed with a green feather.
Canary held out a yellow feather.

Each feather stuck to Peacock's body in a jumble. He had a big coat, but not a pretty one.

"What a mess!" a voice echoed from above. It was the moon shining over the birds in a blue haze.

"Sorry!" the birds said. "We tried to help Peacock."
"Let me finish this job!" the moon laughed.
Moonbeams swirled down and around Peacock in a
magical, mysterious light.
"Now spread out your tail," the moon told Peacock.

All his friends stared in silent amazement. The jumbled feathers on Peacock's body had become a clear, colorful pattern.

And to this day, Peacock displays his feathers in a giant fan—showing everyone how beautiful kindness can be.

Fun Facts about Peacocks

"Proud as a peacock." Have you heard that saying? It means being vain or too proud. But it is not fair to say that the peacock is boastful. He displays his colorful train in a giant fan to catch the eye of a female called a peahen. Peahens like males with flashy feathers. A peahen's feathers are not as large or as colorful as a peacock's.

The peacock and the peahen are peafowls. They are part of the pheasant family, which means they are related to turkeys and partridges. They live in forests and eat grains, insects, berries, and seeds. There are two main types of peafowl. The Indian peacock, from India and Sri Lanka, has blue feathers on his body. This is the ornamental bird most people recognize as the peacock. The green peafowl native to Southeast Asia, while still beautiful, looks a little different. There is also a species of peafowl that live in the Congo.

An Indian peahen is drab brown and can blend into the bushes. This helps her to hide while she sits on her eggs. The babies are called peachicks and both sexes look like their mother at first. Young peacocks don't develop their colorful feathers for a couple of years. Peafowl sleep in trees.

The elegant train of a peacock can be over five feet with a hundred feathers. Still, the peacock is able to fly. His long back feathers come out easily. If a leopard or other predator grabs his train, the bird can escape, leaving his blue-eyed feathers behind.

Indian peafowls have been imported since ancient times. Egyptian Pharaohs, King Solomon in the Bible, and the Greek king Alexander the

Great owned them. Today, they live on farms, in parks, and in zoos all over the world. They can adapt to different environments.

The peacock is the national bird of India and appears in Hindu mythology. The Yazidi people of Iraq honor a deity called "The Peacock Angel." In Greek myth, the eyespots in a peacock's feathers are associated with Zeus' wife, Hera. She is said to have taken one hundred eyes from a creature named Argus and put them into the tail of her favorite bird, the peacock. Christians consider the peacock a symbol of immortality. The majestic bird has been portrayed widely in art and its feathers have been used in elaborate hats.

To learn more about the Indian peafowl, you can visit the websites of the Smithsonian National Zoo or the San Diego Zoo.

 # About the Story

There are tales from around the world depicting a time before birds had warm colorful feathers. "How Buzzard Got His Feathers" from the Iroquois is a famous one. But *Feathers for Peacock* is my original creation. Authors often take a pinch from one story and a pinch from another to create something entirely new. The tale that inspired me the most for *Feathers for Peacock* was "El Mucaro" from Puerto Rico, retold by Derek Burrows in his audiocassette *Afro-Caribbean Animal Folktales*. In this tale, an owl borrows feathers but doesn't return them. For my story, I changed the bird to a peacock and developed a theme of generosity.

—J.J.

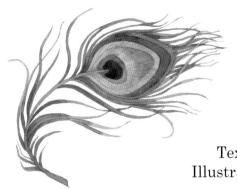

To Madelyn Rosenberg—a very kind friend. ~JJ

For Clive Sefton and family, with much love. ~HC

Feathers for Peacock

Text © 2016 Jacqueline Jules
Illustrations © 2016 Helen Cann

Wisdom Tales is an imprint of World Wisdom, Inc.

Library of Congress Cataloging-in-Publication Data

Names: Jules, Jacqueline, 1956- author. | Cann, Helen, 1969- illustrator.
Title: Feathers for peacock / by Jacqueline Jules ; illustrated by Helen Cann.
Description: Bloomington, Indiana : Wisdom Tales, [2016] | Summary: Relates
how through the generosity of birds of all shapes and sizes Peacock was
given the biggest, most colorful feather coat of all. |
Includes bibliographical references.
Identifiers: LCCN 2015040679 | ISBN 9781937786533 (casebound : acid-free paper)
Subjects: | CYAC: Peacocks--Fiction. | Birds--Fiction. | Feathers--Fiction. |
Generosity--Fiction.
Classification: LCC PZ7.J92947 Fe 2016 | DDC [E]--dc23
LC record available at http://lccn.loc.gov/2015040679

Printed in China on acid-free paper.

Production Date: December 2015,
Plant & Location: Printed by 1010 Printing International Ltd.,
Job/Batch#: TT15110063

For information address Wisdom Tales, P.O. Box 2682,
Bloomington, Indiana 47402-2682
www.wisdomtalespress.com